MW00979324

With love and a hug for Mara!

Library of Congress Cataloging-in-Publication Data available.

ISBN 0-590-48061-8

Copyright © 1995 by Karen Gundersheimer.
All rights reserved.
Published by Scholastic Inc., 555 Broadway, New York, NY 10012.
CARTWHEEL BOOKS is a registered trademark of Scholastic Inc.

12 11 10 9 8 7 6 5 4 3 2 1   5 6 7 8 9/9 0/0

Printed in Singapore

First Scholastic printing, April 1995

Find Cat

Wear Hat

by Karen Gundersheimer

Cartwheel ·B·O·O·K·S· ®

SCHOLASTIC INC.

New York   Toronto   London   Auckland   Sydney

Bang POT

Wash DUCK

Shake RATTLES

Pull TRUCK

Eat COOKIE

Kiss DOLL

Smell FLOWER

Roll BALL

Read BOOK

Count BLOCKS

Drink JUICE

Open BOX

Find CAT

Wear HAT

Hug FRIEND

The End!